T0128823

THE BENEFITS OF A BULLY

THE BENEFITS OF A BULLY

L.A. Kendrick

iUniverse®

THE BENEFITS OF A BULLY

This is a work of fiction. All of the characters, names, incidents,
organizations, and dialogue in this novel are either the products
of the author's imagination or are used fictitiously.

iUniverse books may be ordered through booksellers or by contacting:

iUniverse
1663 Liberty Drive
Bloomington, IN 47403
www.iuniverse.com
1-800-Authors (1-800-288-4677)

ISBN: 978-1-4917-9306-0 (sc)
ISBN: 978-1-4917-9307-7 (e)

Library of Congress Control Number: 2016904838

Print information available on the last page.

iUniverse rev. date: 04/21/2016

Dequavius Weaver
March 20, 1998-March 21, 2014

A brilliant young man who left us too soon,
you are painfully missed Brother Bear!

CONTENTS

CHAPTER 1

Well, I will start off by telling you from a kid's point of view about the weird creepy crawly things that freak us out. Hey, they even used to freak you adults out. I was about eight, my mom and I were headed home for a great night of pizza grubbing, and watching horror movies. My dad was away on a road trip, now for some strange reason mom took a wrong turn; I was in the back seat reading a good scary book. I was way into the whole Mothman, Werewolf, Zombie thing, I always wondered if they were real.

"When it got a bit foggy on the road the tire blew out or something my mom was really upset good thing my dad had shown her how to change the tire. I tried to get out and help but she said to get back into the car, the strange thing is that she had a puzzled look on her face and she kept looking around I guess to make sure everything was safe. Well as safe as it could be, you could only see a few feet in front of your face."

"Mom was working pretty fast and I felt the car lifting over to the left a little, I felt bad not helping, my dad always told me to help ladies and especially mom. Felt like I was letting him down, but I had to respect my mother talking back was never tolerated in my household. She had the tire on I could see her wipe her forehead. Then my dog Roscoe started growling and looking towards the back of the car. My mother looking back too much, straining hard to peer through the fog, I looked back over the seat asking Roscoe what was "wrong. When suddenly

1

a high pitch screech broke through the fog, it was spooky I peeked over the back seat and could see something moving back and forth in the fog. I yelled to my mother get in the car as I quickly opened the door Roscoe streaked out of the car as if going to protect my mother.

"He stood by her side growling, and barking, again I tried to get out with the Little Slugger aluminum bat that my mother keeps in the car; she said it's for protection. Again she says to stay in the car but, this time, she seemed angry as she looked at me, in a blink she was knocked down and screaming but Roscoe was in the mixed fighting really hard as the door slammed shut on me."

"Well, this time, I was not staying put, that's my mom out there fighting for her life. She crawled back to the back of the car as Roscoe bought her a little time. I could barely see the thing but I hit it in the head as hard as I could, it yelled out turned and looked at me, its eyes glowing yellow. Roscoe again was on that thing. Roscoe was a big Great Dane and very mean when it came to my family. It knocked Roscoe off after I saw this I ran to my mother, this thing crawled under the car. I pulled my mother out from under the car as, it came to get us, but mom pepper sprayed it. Boy, the noise it made, we got out from under the car and it continued to follow. As soon as it got close I kicked the car jack and the car came crashing down on it."

"It was pinned and screaming, Roscoe tore into it again, I got the spare gas can we keep in the car as the thing tore whatever part was pinned off. It stood up and Roscoe tackled it, knocking it down, wasn't much gas in the can but I threw it on the thing. I grabbed one of the road flares my mother had put out while she was changing the tire, I called Roscoe off and threw the flare on the creature it was set in a blaze. It was really trying to get the fire off of it, but it took off into the fog yelling in pain."

"My mom quickly grabbed me by the arm and jumped into the car, she yelled to Roscoe, he jumped in and she drove off very fast. She didn't even bother to pick up the car jack. I looked out the back window but all I could see was the fire as it slowly faded into the fog as we got away."

"Mom cried all the way home as Roscoe licked her face seemed like he was trying to tell her that it was going to be ok. I was scared, angry and curious about what that thing was and had my question about if monsters are real, yep they really are!"

"Well that was about three years ago, and yep I still love horror novels. Even at the ripe old age of twelve well at least I will be twelve in a few weeks. There has got to be something that can help me figure that thing out, I've searched the Internet but mom has child block stuff on so I don't get into any grown up stuff. Sometimes though when my dad is away so much I really do feel like the man of the house. He leaves a bunch of good books around for me to read, he likes me to challenge my mind.

"Now here I am at Tubman Middle School, about to go to second class. We have this bully Dexter he loves beating up the scared little guys. What I don't get is why they don't stand up for themselves; they want someone to do it for 'em."

"Well that won't be me he will beat on; glad my dad taught me how to stand up for myself. He's got a kid now pounding him on the playground, I guess I should break it up since no one else is they just keep chanting the famous "Fight, Fight,". Poor Sterling well here goes, oh, by the way, I'm Sedale, Sedale Johnson.

"And this, my friends, is what I believe my dad means when he says bullies have their benefits!"

CHAPTER 2

"Ok, Dexter he's had enough let 'em go!" He seemed a bit shocked that I said this to him in front of everybody they all looked a bit shocked too. Why no kid would dare stand up to Dexter and live to tell the tale. But he actually let Sterling go how about that?

"So I guess you wanna take his place huh Butt sniffer?" Dexter asks.

"Nah just don't see the point of beating him up anymore he's half your size dude not mention you look like you need to stop eaten everybody's lunch. Your skinny jeans are screaming for mercy!" I say to him he gets mad as everyone starts laughing.

"Well, you won't be smiling when I knock your teeth outta your dumb face Dirt Licker." Dexter says as he comes charging at me like a mad bull, his first mistake.

"I step to the left and right just like my dad taught me he's throwing punches wildly left, right and then all over the place. Holy cow it's just like my dad showed me he is tiring himself out. He's breathing like a rabid dog."

"Ok Dexter as much as I would love to kick your can all over the playground, you are not gonna lay a finger on me! I'm just gonna let you tire your weird skinny jeans out. Plus you might wanna take a knee and fix your ridiculous hair… Parrot puncher!"

"Man he is really gasping for air. I think he might hurl, look out everybody he's gonna blow. His face becomes white as a ghost and then he explodes.

"The area is filled with eeeewwwws, and every other sound a kid can muster, well let me make him an offer to stop bullying."

"You had enough?" I ask as he stumbles to get his balance then he let's loose a nasty loud fart that has cleared most of the playground.

"Man, I'm gonna wail on you so hard!" Dexter yells.

"Ok well I heard that you are the best at the video game 'Kage of the Katana' well I'm pretty good too my friend. We can set up a game challenge at the local youth center, there's already a tournament coming up. Now if I beat you, you gotta stop beating on the kids for a year!" I say to him.

"What if I win, what do I get out of it?" Dexter questions.

"Well if you win, you get to keep beating on kids smaller than you and I'll give you my allowance for a year!" I respond to him.

"You are so dead, cake head I've neva been beaten in that game, I'm gonna love taking your money chump. Name the time and date!" Dexter says to a team of ooohs from the remaining kids as if to add to the drama.

"This weekend 10:00 am get ready Freddy!" As we do the playground stare down thing, the bell rings for class to start and Dexter takes the challenge but not before he slaps Sterling hard on the back of the head!

"Beat you later Sterile Sterling!" Dexter says as he leaves for class.

"Dude you have got to stand up for yourself, you can't keep letting him beat on you and take your stuff everyday!" I tell Sterling as I help him up.

"Well Sedale, everybody can't fight or be smart like you that guy is scary he once stuffed a kid in a locker and glued his butt crack closed. Man, that is hardcore!" Sterling answered.

"He looked really scared at this point so, I say to him what my dad tells me all the time about Bullies."

"Bullies are good, they teach us a few things, about life. For example, a good parent prepares their child for facing

5

the world without them holding their hands. Because a good parent knows that they can't always be there to do that sorta of thing like fight their kids battles. It's not fair but neither is life he would tell me. You are either gonna stand and face life's challenges or live on your knees and get walked all over and used. Be a Sheep or a Warrior?" I say to him.

"Wow that's pretty deep, I never looked at it that way, heck I never heard it that way. But that guy puts the fear in me!" Sterling replies.

"Stand your ground and take the power of the Bully away, I'll beat him this weekend and then I'll show you how to defend yourself without lifting a finger. Trust me when I say this there are worst things to fear in this world than bullies!" I say to Sterling as we head for class he laughs a bit and I have to stop and get my belongings that I left back.

"Go ahead man I'll catch up, man that kids' got a lot to learn." Oh snap, where did I leave my backpack?

"I start looking around for where I had it last and I don't see it, then a strange man approaches me with my pack in his hand. He looks serious, no smile, black suit with a white hat can't figure out who he is or what is this joker doing on school grounds with no adults around."

"Thanks, Mister that's my backpack can I have it?" I ask the man my parents always say never talk to strangers, but if you do be careful and respectful. This guy never says a word just looks at me very strange, made me a bit uncomfortable.

"So sir may I please have my pack? I gotta get to class, and I have homework that I have got to turn in."

"He still says nothing but he slowly hands me my pack, I thank the weirdo and walk away I can't help but look over my shoulder as I get far enough away. As I turn to do so however he, of course, is not there imagine that. So I stop and look around for the strange man in the black suit."

Nowhere to be found man that makes me a little nervous there are a lot of crazy people in the world, let me get to class.

I get pats on the back from the kids and they are already making bets for the epic video game battle this weekend. Now I'm wondering what grade I got on yesterday's pop quiz if I score well then I'll get that new video game controller for an early birthday gift, well not really I'm gonna buy it with the extra allowance. Oh ok for the moment of truth the teacher is calling role, and now for the grade.

YES, an A, I smile ear-to-ear, sigh I look around the room and hear the groans of bad grades. I get a tap on my back its Sterling probably about to brag about his grade or something lets see.

"Ok Sterling what's up?" I ask he has got geek written all over his face.

"I got an A+ what did you get? I bet I smoked your grade?" Sterling boasts.

"I got an A, but you see that, if you took that same attitude that you are taking you wouldn't get bullied wait yes you would, I'm still tougher than you. Dexter wants to keep you lord of homework, look at him over there he looks really mad, must have failed the test. He is really rubbing his head like that's gonna make his grade better."

"I know right he should spend more time studying instead of bullying!" Sterling says as we both laugh.

"What's so ha ha Dweebs, I know you are not making fun of my grade?" Dexter asks.

"We don't know what you made on your test but your reaction just said it all. Chill out you gonna be even more disappointed this weekend!" I say to him.

"I'm so gonna love beating you down and taking your money, and Sterling snot cruncher you're first to get punched on my list!" Dexter says.

"Mister Pulgie, do you have something that you want to share with the rest of the class or would detention make you feel better about your poor grade?" the teacher asks, to a class of snickers from the other kids.

"No Ms. Terry, just thinking out loud!" Dexter responds.

"Very good then, class open your books to page 131, let's go over the answers to the pop quiz!" Ms. Terry says. While she begins the lessons I go to daydreaming about monsters and zombies so maybe I need to get my mind on the lesson at hand. Nah I'll just keep dreaming.

The class gets about half way done and I glance out the window thinking about summertime and that's a ways off from now. To my shock there is that same weird guy in the black suit and white hat, now I'm getting just a lil' freaked out because he is looking… well in my direction I just can't see his eyes because of the glasses. I turn to Sterling to get a witness.

"Hey Sterling look very slowly out the window and tell me what you see, now I'm really speaking in a low voice because the teacher is talking, and I don't wanna get into trouble."

"Don't look too quick I don't want him to leave." I say to him.

"Who to leave what are you talking about crazy cooler? They got places for things that you are going through, I see dead people!" Sterling says with his hands up like Frankenstein's Monster.

"Just look out the window and stop being an idiot, do it now if you don't mind," I say to him and he does. Slowly his face frowns up and his answer is?

"Yep crazy just like I said there ain't nobody out there but the janitor, he's throwing trash into the dumpster. That's it, was I supposed to be looking for that ghoul junk that you read about all the time?" Sterling responds in a low voice.

"That's it are you messing with me?" I look out the window and what do you know he is gone again, boy do I really feel stupid.

"He was just there!" I say to Sterling then the teacher gets involved.

"Mr. Sedale, Mr. Sterling do you two gentlemen have something more important or do you want to continue this in detention?" Ms. Terry yells her voice really scared us?

"No ma'am just, talking about what you are going over." I tried to cover for us.

"Well if you have any questions you need to address me, okay?"

"Yes Ms. Terry, you got it." We just dodged detention but I still don't know who that guy is I can't wait to find out.

"We dodged detention didn't we on that one?" Sterling asks looking scared as usual. He's never been in any trouble other than the beating that is Dexter. I think that won't count against him though.

"Yeah I know." I reply to him anyway then I just shut up and listen to the teacher but I'm keeping my eye on that window. Maybe freaky creep guy will show again. I'm gonna snap a picture with my camera phone this time.

"School is out for the day and I'm glad ready to get home, get ready for the weekend battle against Dexter. I might stop buy the store and get some junk food for the afternoon cartoons. There is a store that serves great burgers and fries, plus their milk shakes are always on point. Also I think that the new issue of Creature catalog magazine is due out, I'm gonna love this weekend yeah!"

"I skip the bus ride home so I can get my feel of the nice autumn air; besides I only live a few blocks over, I don't wanna be one of those fat kids they are always talking about on T.V. I watch adults they seem to always be talking about money and bills glad I don't have that worry right now, only thing I have is this need to stop the grumbling in my stomach. Why did I skip lunch?"

CHAPTER 3

"I'm here finally made it to Mr. Irving's store, best burgers in town I run in fast so that I can place an order this is one of the only times of the day where you can actually get in without the big crowd. This place is what I believe is called a historical landmark been in his family and the town for a long time. Now to place my order."

"Good afternoon Mr. Irving, I will have the Creature crusher combo burger with cheese hold the bacon, extra ketchup, and a vanilla shake please." He has many colorful names for his meal originals.

"Son where do you put it all, you can't weight more than 40 or 60 pounds at the most. But it will be right up!" Mr. Irving says.

"Mr. Irving seems to be really into the news right now. I'm just gonna look at some of the historical pictures on the walls, a bunch of famous people have been through this place."

"Excuse me Mr. Irving, but have you heard about the video game challenge this weekend between me and some other kids. We know you always referee, these sorta things?" I ask as he still looks at the T.V. set, but still he manages to flip burgers as if he was using the force.

"Huh? Oh yeah will be there, word travels fast here, and I hear that you are doing this for a noble cause to make Dexter a non-factor in the bullying department. I say well good for you!"

as he points his spatula in my direction and then his attention goes back at the T.V.

"I think so if you stand for nothing you'll fall for anything and this guy needs to be put in his place so bad!"

"Now my young friend, despite what you hear on the T.V… Bullies do have their place in this world. Now if it's a one-on-one bully fight, that's ok you're going to take bumps and bruises in life, the sooner you learn this, the better you are later in life. Mom and Dad won't always be there to help, first there's high school, next college they won't be there, then the real world where you get out and find a job and make your own path." Mr. Irving says.

"Bullies will be everywhere in life, they don't just go away but you have to figure out a way to stand your ground you win some, you lose, some but at least you get to keep your dignity. You can't put a price on that let me tell you!" Mr. Irving adds, as he finishes up my order, he's a very smart and cool guy.

"What's that on T.V.? Mr. Irving, you've been looking at it a bunch what's going on Sir?" I ask him he looks away from the set and tells me.

"Well, local kids have been coming up missing like right out of the homes at different times. They've got no leads on who's doing it, and it's got the adults very worried. Here's your order now, you kick his butt tomorrow and be careful on your way home. Thanks to the Internet that whole don't talk to strangers has gone out the window just like most manners. People are crazy in the world." Mr. Irving says as I pay him for the food and leave, and he points to a guy blowing his nose near people eating.

"GROSS, come to think of it… I hardly ever see people covering their mouths when they eat, cough or sneeze. Mr. Irving might be on to something? My parents taught me that manners are very important and that they are building blocks of human character."

"Now I wonder if that man that's been creeping around school has anything to do with the missing kids? I begin to wonder. I thank Mr. Irving and move to get home fast."

"As I make my way home trying to make sure that my food doesn't get too cold, I can't help but wonder what else is out there, and I think about the detectives that I have read about. I really want to be a mystery hunter you know like that guy in the old T.V. series "The Night Stalker" Kolchak I think that's how you say his name. I want to check and see if there are any schools that train for this, here I go again but man I love imagination. Here I come computer."

"When I get home, my mother is looking at the T.V. also, and she looks nervous as she turns to me and begins to question me. Oh boy, what did I do?"

"Young man where have you been, and why didn't you take the bus home don't you know what's been happening out in the town lately it's all over the news. Take the bus home from now on no more shop stopping, stay with a friend. Kids are coming up missing this world is not safe." She really seemed messed up, and I don't blame her after that attack that happened to us three years ago. My mother knows first hand what kinds of terrors lie outside of our doors or imagination. She hardly even lets me go out at night I wish there was something I could do, I want to track that thing down that attacked us but I would need training in tracking."

"I'm gonna enjoy this meal, and the afternoon cartoons then get ready for the Friday night horror fest that's going to be shown later. Life just keeps getting sweeter. While I wait for the sun to set I'll jump on the Internet, to see if there are any colleges that offer the kind of spook trackers that I would love to make my career, never too early to get started on my future."

"Ok found something, Lewis Latimer academy of tracking hmmm let me keep this site on my history link."

"It seems to offer a lot more than I thought it would, weapons use, tracking, deductive reasoning what ever that is and cryptic anthropology are also taught. Sounds like what I've been looking for, I'm going to take down this phone number. Well, enough of that time for the Horror movies and my favorite pepperoni, Italian sausage pizza and lemonade mom really knows how to get the party started right. She's a good woman I'm gonna make her proud some day that's a promise."

"For now, though bring on the Horror, 50's 60's 70's 80's monster mashing all the way up to 2000's YEEEEEEAH, I make it to the 90's then I doze off!"

"OH MY GOSH I over slept the alarm didn't go off, I'm gonna be late for the video game contest. Mom why didn't you wake me, I need to shower!"

"Your alarm did go off, you just didn't hear it, not my responsibility to wake you on the weekend unless you have things that I need you to do; you're a big boy! Sterling is waiting outside for you," my mother says.

"You are so right I need my new controller, my video game gloves, and a shower gotta have a shower can't go smelling like a dead cat. Can't believe she bought the controller for me."

"I jump in the shower the! Ouch the water is too hot now I feel like a boiled lobster, I guess I can brush my teeth in here to cut down on time. I jump out of the shower and comb my hair, deodorant where is the deodorant, under my clothes ok got it. Only 30 minutes until the tournament got to keep moving. Ok now the clothes, shoes ok now I'm ready."

"Bye mom be back in about an hour or two, no time for breakfast!" I try to hurry out before she says…

"Wait one-minute young man take this Turkey bacon and egg white sandwich with you, can't win on an empty stomach!" My mom replies.

"Ok, mom, thanks!" I kiss her on the cheek and rush to my bike outside. Hey, don't hate what's a kiss on the cheek between mother and son we've been through a lot ok.

"Man let's go the fate of the universe lies in your capable hands we can't be late, let's go, go, go!" Sterling yells with excitement he's got a good point time to put the bully down.

"Let's do this." I say to Sterling as we jump on our bikes and zoom to the youth center. We can see that it's packed more than I thought it would be."

"Whoa, this thing is gonna be epic everybody wants the big dummy to fall don't let us down Sedale!" Sterling says.

"Oh, I won't he has this coming in the worst way possible!" I respond as we chain up our bikes and enter the building its filled wall to wall with the games lit up on 60-inch flat screen T.V.s. I sign in and what's this Sterling does the same, curious?

"What are you doing Sterling?" I ask him he has a Devilish grin on his face like some midget mad scientist.

"I will fight for my honor and dignity just like you said I should, this will be my first start you know in case you don't beat him. I am in the battle also just entered online last night. My dad just enrolled me in boxing classes also so I'm going to be set for battle yes Sir." Sterling responds.

"So you don't have any faith in my gaming skills, you know I don't loose in horde mode. I always out last everyone, and you know this. But by all means join the beating that I'm going to dish out." Just then Dexter pops in here we go.

"Well, I see you showed up to get thrashed hard huh mutant?" Dexter says degradingly while popping his knuckles and as normal Sterling gets scared.

"Why wouldn't I show up you don't know what you are up against when I'm done whipping on you in this game I'll buy you some body wash to get that smell of hot mustard and coffee off of you dog lips." I say to him as all the kids around us burst into laughter. Dexter is angry which is what I was aiming for.

"Whatever cat face you're gonna be wearing Sterling's dirty underwear on your head like a stocking cap when I'm done with you." Dexter retorts with his minions laughing trying to boost his confidence. Just then Mr. Irving explains the rules of the tournament.

"Ok ladies and gentlemen, here are the rules: first you will battle horde mode to the final level of 50. Last man standing wins all. If you survive all 50 wave of the Ninja assault, then you will receive the one hundred dollar bonus. There will be no mods or cheat codes allowed if caught you will be DQ'd. Even though we have it set to not allow it, you will still be Dairy Queened. This is a test of integrity and respect so let's keep it clean and get ready for good gaming." Mr. Irving says.

"Wow that was pretty impressive, each kid has a screen to view just like online so that it's just you and your headset. I think I'll take the seat across from Dexter so that he can't distract me. Well there will be five of us in this game and they will fall quick, this game is really intense. The opponents in this game are relentless I need to ask what level this will be played on."

"Mr. Irving what level will this game be played on, not that it matters just wondering?" I ask and everyone goes quite as he gives the meaningful answer.

"INSANE!" Mr. Irving replies and there is a gasp in the room that could shatter windows, the only ones that don't seem the least bit phased is Dexter and I. Maybe because he thinks that I would show a fear weakness, now I have heard that he is one of the best players in town and I guess we will see!

"Scared Sissy?" Dexter asks with a cracked smile on his face!

"Yeah only at what you'll smell like when I beat the deodorant off of you!"

"Yeah Dexter running around here smelling like fish and Kool-Aid, yeah that's you Wexter! Oh boy!" Sterling says with an epic fail attempt at casing Dexter which put a very stupid look on everyone and all that is heard is a high pitched whistle on the mic used by Mr. Irving. It's kinda of funny, though.

"Okay, is everybody ready?" Mr. Irving asks as I look around as most have food and sodas in their hand, and the air is filled with electricity.

"Oh I think we are ready, I say to myself."

"Let's get it to GOOOOOO!!" Mr. Irving yells as the game starts, the screen is filled with the "Kage of the Katana" music and then it's the beginning of level one pretty quickly as we all five tear through the vampires infected ninjas.

We reach level nine and we get our first beat down casualty along with one not continuing. Sally Goldmier was knocked down by a smoke pellet and we couldn't get to her in time as the vampire ninjas did her in. Now level ten.

"We just knocked out wave 20. It took no time but the clock says we've been going at it for about an hour and a half. Time flies when you're having fun and this game is very intense. We lost the guy back on wave 15. I'm surprised that he lasted that long, but I gotta tell ya this donkey boy Dexter is better than I thought he'd be, a lot better. There are only three of us left as we battle on with the baddies."

"Can't remember the last time I had this much fun everybody here is having the time of their lives. I notice, as there is a break in the game as it adds up the score and level. My dad always says savor the small moments in life cause before you know it life will throw you into adulthood and it will all be "gonna."

"Oh D.M.C game is starting back up. FOCUS TIME!"

"We battled all the way to wave 40 then 45 and at that moment, it happened.

Sterling got it handed to him because of a hard head."

"Ok, wave 46 butt germs we are on no man's land, Sterling don't be stupid I'm watching you make some really stupid crap moves. You cost me this game trying to save your hairless dog back, and I will personally shove a scorpion up your butt! Got it idiot?" Dexter asks and Sterling has his normal look of fear and yes he was costing us and we just barely all got out of wave 45. I hope that he gets the point this is a team game, even though we can't play that way because of the bet.

"It starts again, I get to my spots and set up garlic and oak grenades, and Dexter does the same down the hallway, but Sterling is running to the other side of the map trying to get weapon supplies. Oh my gosh what a dumb move because now the Vampire ninjas have cut him off from the rest of us, this is what cost the last guy playing, last round he got knocked out of the game he went to save Sterling's beef, and got cooked in the process. Now here he goes again, I can't get to him for the horde is attacking me from all sides."

"Sterling ain't gonna make it this time, and I'm playing for something bigger than his dumb moves boy oh, boy! Maybe I can coach him over to where we are?"

"Sterling cross the bridge I'll give you cover fire, it's clear for a few seconds but they are coming in tough!" I say to him through the headset!

"MOVE NOW!" As he does he tries to make his way over and they swarm him all over and he fights off a few of them.

"I unload with my ultraviolet rounds turn a few vamps into sparklers but then one downs him and he tries to crawl to us; not gonna happen."

"I knew you were a geek burger, but now you're a geek burger with cheese on it how stupid can you be? If you think I'm coming out to save you then you are a dead man! So eat it Shark Belly!" Dexter says as the horde tears Sterling up and his game is over as is the wave. Dexter is laughing hard at what just happened to Sterling; well to tell you the truth it was kinda funny hearing his character scream like a woman. Dexter is showing that he is a good player in this game too bad he's a bully and now I have to bring him down a notch.

"The two of us battle on with a close call here and there for the both of us so no clear advantage but I do love the feel of my new controller. I feel great about my chances and I won't give up but it's time, wave 50!"

"Well badger butt you ain't half bad at this game I thought you'd suck I gotta admit, but that don't mean that you are going to win I got this hands down and your money for a year!" Dexter says.

"You believe it cow kidney's, you ain't seen nothing yet the look on your face says you've never seen wave 50 we have to survive until the sun comes out in the game. Then the ceiling explodes and the sunlight rains down on them and vaporizes them. It is a smooth ending." I respond to Dexter to his shock he tries to come back with an intelligent answer.

"That's only rumor you got that off the Internet I'm sure because only one person has made it to that level but you aren't him so don't try and play me. They say he was just guessing and that he never made it either, but I will this day count on it!" Dexter says.

"Yeah but you'll be looking at me take the prize money and glory, and the bragging rights, bro I'm about to own!" I say this with total confidence because I know what I'm about to do, trust me. This is a tale told from my minds eye. I heard my dad make that statement a bunch.

"We are here kids the final wave 50, winner takes all and bragging rights so if the light is too bright from these two stars then go and put your sunglasses oooooooooon!" Mr. Irving yells.

"You gotta love his presentation like he is announcing the beginning of a heavy weight-boxing match. Everyone is yelling and screaming with excitement."

"Well you know what let's go Dexter, I say to myself. It's go time.

My hands begin to sweat they sorta do that when I get excited or nervous. Dexter notices this and tosses me some powder to stop my hands from sweating."

"Well, I want to see the end of this game, gonna be tough to do that without help so apply generously Donkey boy!" Dexter says as he leans over after his bad toss of the powder to me.

"We enter the wave and I've never seen a more realistic video game surrounding, the spider webs, water dripping from the celling and the torches that light the corridor. I look over at Dexter and he looks just as amazed as I am. I set up and then look to the secret spot where they say a powerful nitro ultra violet bomb is. I get to it quick before Dexter can see me then I plant it, where I can hide if I need to set it off without taking to much damage."

I have been sloppy but the match has started and I hear a gun shot and then I turn to see ash and light. Wow, Dexter has just saved me from a rogue Vamp, he could have let me die and won the match what do you know. I can't believe I was that dumb, dang it!

"That's one you owe me I don't wanna beat you by some stupid mistake, now I want to beat you without any excuses!" Dexter responds, and as soon as he finishes he takes his attention off the game and a vamp drops down incasing him and about to finish him off. I move in between them and attach a garlic grenade onto the vamp and shove it back, and help Dexter up as the creature explodes.

"Even Steven, I feel the same don't wanna beat you that way, where is the sport in that it would be like the silly Modder's that play online and say they're good!" I tell him as I pick his character up we move into positions on the same side, hey it's the only way to survive: no running out or being a running Rambo, just got to cover each others back.

"We battle hard didn't even realize it's been five hours playing this game, watch as the grenades we planted blew up, scattering the vamps all over the place. I use my Katana and Dexter uses his garlic arrow cross bow boy this is fun."

"Cool huh fart blaster, tell me when you've had such a great time here I've been hating you all this time now I'm starting to like you!" Dexter yells to me. Hmp, weird to hear that we've been enemies since I can remember.

"I know right? Here I thought you where only good at sniffing goat butts, hard to believe you are the scourge of the school. Close to then end of this game now, though! LOOK OUT!" I yell to him as he is swarmed I cover him with ultra violet rounds and he rolls out of the way and behind cover, he then picks up a sword and starts cutting the vamps down. But they force us back towards the bomb I have planted.

"We are getting overrun, these things won't stop coming, they are crawling all over the walls, floor, and ceiling concentrate on the roof, I got the ceiling."

I say to him. We take a lot of damage and hits, but the wave should be over just a few more kills.

"Got it they like the way these rounds taste, WELL COME ON I'VE GOT MORE!" Dexter yells to the vamps and I can't help but admire his battle spirit.

Just then the boss vamp comes in comes, he jumps to pounce me but I cut him with my Katana that after leveling up it has a magical cutting property and he is finished with a few swipes.

Dexter is not so lucky because now he has two of these huge mutant vamps on him, he kills one and the other is showing him the business side of his fist. He still manages to get to my side of the room.

"We have to make it to that divider; I've got a surprise for them. We can't hold this point any more!" I say to Dexter.

"You're right Weird Willie; let's battle on over there then!" Dexter replies as we fight over to the point of no return.

Game enemy count shows there is a secret horde coming. We battle hard but we can't stop them, so I turn to my last resort. We jump over the blockade after I set the bomb in motion 10-second count down. Out of nowhere Dexter goes down and I follow. We are both shocked because now we can't get the other up. We were struck by the Mega Vamp dude we never saw coming.

"Oh, crap we are not gonna finish this wave we came too far for it to end like this!" Dexter says as I feel his anger and frustration, I think it's over for the both of us but then all of a sudden the bomb goes off killing most of the vamps but the biggest one is staggered as the ceiling caves in and Dexter's character energy runs out just as the sunlight fries the big baddie and everything left in the room.

"A hush goes over the youth center as my character stands just seconds before my energy taps out and the game awards me the victor of "Kage of the Katana horde mode." The center is filled with cheers from everyone present, even Dexter walks up to me through all of the noise and confusion and begins to congratulate me.

"Dude heck of a game you got my respect now!" He slaps me on the back and raises my hand pointing at me. All I can hear is my name being cheered.

Sterling is all too happy with what just happened. He won't be picked on for a full year. Now I'm about to get paid with the prize money. I look to find Dexter and he is walking out of the building but he gives me a thumbs-up on his way out.

What do you know, a bully does have a lot of unseen benefits? When you stand up to them, you take away their power, but when you beat them fair and square you earn their respect. My dad says that the ultimate bully is life, which is the one bully no one can protect you from. You can only try to prepare for because it will be there as long as a person lives, this bully will knock you down and dare you to get up but because I have strong parents, I'll take that dare. This is an early life lesson that nobody here will ever forget. Well if they get the message.

As I receive the prize money, I also get a nice sized trophy, this will look good in my bedroom. I grab a cup of punch and sit back enjoying my moment of triumph. I sit around for about 30 minutes then I take my earnings and trophy and head on home with Sterling jumping up and down. He is so happy that there will be no more bullying this year.

"Man that game was epic, I thought you were done when you both where knocked down and the celling fell. I thought you where done just like Dexter man I almost filled my pants with brown mud, but you pulled it off." Sterling says, elated.

"I know, right, I thought the same, but I guess the good lord was with me this day," I say to Sterling as we get to the mid point of his house and mine he rides to his house on his bike. It's been a long day I look up at the sky and smile I make my way home to the front door. "It sure feels good to win this today," I sigh. Time to show my mom, She's gonna be proud. "Hey, mom! Check this out!"

CHAPTER 4

What a weekend, glad to be back at school. Wait did I just say that I'm glad to be back at school? Scratch that, what I really meant is that I want to see if Dexter keeps his word, all the kids are coming up high fiving, hand shaking, and patting me on the back for a job well done against the ultimate bully.

Hmmm-pretty cool! Now to class I have a few classes with Sterling and Dexter this is one of them first period. There is Sterling sitting proud, wonder what he has to say this time?

"Dude you rocked this weekend, so much that you are going to be voted class president in the up and coming election," Sterling boasts, but something seems missing today?

"Dexter ain't here today, wonder where he is? Has anyone seen him?"

"Nope, don't know and who cares, he probably jumped on the first plane to China he can't show his face around here I bet after that thrashing you gave him!" Sterling adds.

"Yeah but this doesn't sound like him, I think he has perfect attendance he has never missed a day of school the last two years. Partially so that he can bully everybody, and you can't be an effective bully if you miss school!" I say to Sterling.

"Well, good riddance to 'em I won't miss that chimp!" Sterling says. I can't shake the feeling that something is wrong as the teacher calls role. It really is strange looking at that empty seat where Dexter sits normally. I wonder what the deal is?

Well, we go through lunch which was pizza day it wasn't that bad and, the other boring classes that don't peak imagination, there has got to be more out there for a young mind willing to advance himself. Now I sound like Mr. Spock from "Star Trek" the whole day is gone and there still was no sign of Dexter. Well, Sterling and I go outside; school is done for the day. So the question is again asked.

"Still no Dexter, man I wonder what is going on this is so not like him and we have had a lot of missing children lately. It's been all over the news, haven't you been watching?"

"Watching, smotching, no one would want that mean wood booger. That dude tormented me for as long as I can remember, man I had nightmares about him he was dressed like a killer clown chasing me through this school but it was empty! It was so creepy and real so forget that bag of rat-spit glad he's gone!" Sterling says, man I didn't realize how much Dexter affected his life. I can't expect to understand what it must have been like.

"Sorry bro if he was this bad I wonder what his home life was like and what would make a cat act like that?" I reply to Sterling but just then that creepy black hat guy steps out from nowhere it seems and, this time, Sterling can see him clearly!

"Who is that creep trolling around here; he shouldn't be here he's not one of the staff," Sterling says and his voice is shaking.

'That's the guy I told you that has been walking around the schoolyard, I told you to look the other day. When you did though he was gone, and you called me crazy, well now welcome to the crazy club!" I remind Sterling.

"We need to tell the bus driver when he pulls up wait here comes the driver!" Sterling responds. I never take my eye off the troller don't want him to vanish into thin air like he has done so many times before. We run to the driver and tell him about the stranger, finally, some one will see him. The driver steps off the bus and what do ya know the creep is gone, again. The driver looks at us sorta upset.

"What are you boys up to stop wasting time and get on the bus," the driver says to us.

"But there was a tall weird man out there for real no games, Mr. Hunter!" Sterling tries to explain.

"Yeah whatever get on!" Mr. Hunter the driver says. We do and he drives us home or close to it. Sterling and I never say a word about it on the way home; as we get off the bus we look at each other one last time and shake our heads. We then walk away to our houses, I get in and say hello to my mom and she's got dinner going, smells good too, she's glued to the reality T.V. show that's on, I really don't get those shows adults and their drama!

"We finish dinner she asks me about school like she always does, I give her the basic kid answer, it was okay. I help her place the dishes in the sink I then grab the trash and take it to the Herbie Curbie, man the sun set really looks nice, a bit chilly, though. I get back in the house and hit the bathroom for a shower, nothing like a hot one. I step out and dry off when the phone rings. I'm hoping it's my dad, but it's Sterling."

"What's up Ster?" I ask him he takes a few seconds to answer.

"You know I'm kinda wondering what happened to Dexter now after seeing that man and my parents are talking about all the missing kids popping up lately. They seem worried," Sterling answers.

"Mine are too, so am I maybe he'll show up tomorrow and we can see how he really took that loss last weekend?" I reply to him.

"Well I'm not a monster and it was a bit weird not seeing him today. He still makes me sick, though," Sterling says.

"I'm gonna read this book 'Destiny vs. Chaos' and call it a night it's a pretty good book. Guess I'll catch you in the morning. Oh and try not to get disappeared, okay?" I say to him as we hang up.

"I want to read the first couple of chapters to my new book, but I'm really tired, okay? Headphones, flashlight, and book well let's get to it! Oh, I think I need to say a prayer for my dad, those missing kids, and Dexter. AMEN!"

"Next day at school I'm looking around, still no Dexter, well he'll turn up I hope. The teacher again calls role, and to my surprise no Sterling today. I look to his seat and he is a no show. Now I'm a bit worried and to tell you the truth scared. The other kids also start mumbling about our missing classmates."

"The class ends and the teacher instructs us all to be careful on our way home and then she calls out, "Class dismissed". It's the weekend and my birthday is Saturday, but it is hard to get excited about it with my missing friends."

"As I make my way home, I get off the bus and turn the corner for my house, and out of nowhere there is the creepy guy, and I run right into him.

I'm a bit angry and I do what my parents always tell me never to do. I talk to a stranger."

"Mr. what is your problem you keep popping up everywhere before you started showing up kids didn't go missing. Explain yourself don't just stand there staring like the weirdo you are, I know you have something to do with my missing friends!" He says nothing but just stands there looking, a blank expression on his face with sunglasses on.

"I take off running for home, I look back once and the creepo waves at me and points like he has a gun and fires a fake warning shot. I get to my house out of breath and tell my mom what just happened. She calls the police and when they get to my house I give a detailed description of the man. Gotta say something is wrong when adults get cops in on a thing. They take the report and leave and I explain to my mother about

Sterling and Dexter not being in school. She says maybe they are on vacation because she saw Sterling's family leaving early this morning. I think to myself okay, I tell her I'm not hungry, I go to my room and put on my MP3 player and listen to music. Man are my eyes heavy!"

Trying to fight sleep, wow that was quick the moon is out. It's huge, oh snap! Ha ha maybe because I dozed off or something, I'll figure…. It all out in the morning my birthday's tomorrow, can't wait to see what…

"BLAM, BLAM, BLAM that's the sound my alarm makes as It wakes me out of a really deep sleep and strange dream. Man, I hit the floor hard it's still ha ha as I try to unroll myself from the covers. Let me get the toothbrush working and the shower going, today is my day the big 1-2."

'Cake, ice cream, new video games, oh I know a telescope, night vision goggles you know the ones that make everything all green at night. I rack my brain trying to figure out what I'll get today. I hop out of the shower, make sure my face is clean, no eye crust."

"Now to the mom down stairs bet she has got something nice just waiting for me. To my shock what do I see it's like a nightmare!'

"NOOOOOOOOOOO! MOM WHAT IS HE DOING HERE HE'S THE CREEPY GUY I TOLD YOU ABOUT YESTERDAY, RUN MOM, RUN!!!" I say to her as I grab a baseball bat. She leaves it in the corner for protection, I gotta get this bum outta here before he gets us like I know he did Dexter and Sterling. But I'm surprised that my mom is not moving away from him, what is going on here?

"Sedale calm down and come sit down I have something to tell you!" My mother says, man I don't want to sit with that troll.

"No mom this guy is bad and he should leave, everyday, the other missing kids I know that he is behind it. I…"

"SEDALE SIT DOWN NOW LIKE I TOLD YOU!" My mother says in a tone I rarely hear her use, at this point I don't mess around I move because she is serious now. I slowly move into the room never taking my eye off the weirdo bro, and then he begins to tell me an amazing story. Again let me remind you I can't tell this story with all the grown folks big words. This story is coming from my child's eyes and mind, cool huh? Because lord knows how grown people like to use those big hard to understand words, I think it makes them feel special I guess.

"My name is Washington Brown, I am here because kids like you are needed, I've been watching you for a while now and you have what it takes for our rather lucrative organization. What I mean by that is you have shown a passion for the unknown, you searched the internet database that has a link that alerts us when young people like yourself show interest. You have shown tremendous cognitive, deductive, on the spot breaking down of a situation, and above all leadership skills.

"You want to know obviously about the things that go bump in the night, well you and your mother have already seen a small percent of why, well truth be told, the thing that you saw is part of a phenomenon of why people go missing. These things must be hunted, trapped and contained. What we provide is a school for the next generation of cryptic, supernatural, and paranormal hunters," Washington Brown says. I'm really shocked, they do have a school, there is training, and there is a life that I can help make the world safe. Boy, oh boy I'm trying hard not to smile right now some birthday present huh?

"So there is a place that I can go to train and be like a superhero or something? How long will I need to be gone for and what will be my studies again?" I asked him as he smiles for the first time since I've seen him wandering around.

"You will be sent through a six-month training exercise, it will be intense, I will have to warn you. There is a place for training in Ft. Leonard Wood MS where you will be sent through like a boot camp, it will prepare you and other candidates for this line of work. Also, I have to warn you not all pass this test only the best of the best, you will get up early and go to be late, run, do push-ups, sit-ups until you collapse some days.

"You and the others will become best friends with obstacle courses, and rope climbing, 5-mile hikes, and sleep will not be your ally when you embark on this journey. The second half of your training will be the identification and understanding of everything we have on file. Aliens, Witches, Ghosts, Monsters and these are just the start; I tell you believe it or not these are just the tips of the unforeseen iceberg. We have to keep these things from spilling over, and taking over humanity," Mr. Brown says.

"So kids control this whole thing, you have kids fighting these monsters and other stuff?" I ask I don't know how kids can stop those things because that one almost got me and my mom, it was strong and fast.

"No, you are the future, we have the Apex teams that are comprised of adults that start off like you, but go through years of training and are sent on specialized monitored assignments until they prove that they can handle the field. Usually once they reach adult status the training wheels come off, and they take on unmonitored assignments but report to the higher ups. At the point that you pass the initial training assignments, you will be able to sign up for classes that interest you most in this elite field," Mr. Brown replies.

"Mom, what do you think, would you let me go would you let me?" I ask as she smiles at me.

"I've already signed the consent forms and, they will be providing you with better education than you are getting at the public school you are in right now so it's up to you, and your dad gives his approval also," my mother responds.

"So are you in, Mr. Johnson, we could sure use someone like you, or I should say the world could use you and other?" Mr. Brown asks I feel butterflies in my stomach but I tell you that this is what I have been dreaming of for a very long time. I give my answer.

"YES SIR WHEN DO I START?" I say like I really know what I'm getting into but I welcome the challenge as I jump to my feet, like I had a rocket under my seat.

"Monday if it is all right with your mother, we will give you time to pack and get things in order. You can't tell your friends about where you are going," he says to me like I have any friends left to tell, well, any important ones anyway.

"I have a question if you don't mind me asking, sir, I have had some friends go missing do you know where they are?" I ask as if he could know his answer is kind of surprising, though.

"Who knows? Maybe when you start and finish your training, you will be able to find or run into them yourself. Good day, Mrs. Johnson, Sedale we will be seeing you Monday, oh, and Happy Birthday!" He finishes as he grabs his hat and walks out the front door. I look at my mother and she stands up with arms wide open.

"Congratulations, son, and looks like you will be getting even with that thing that attacked us that night. Nice Birthday surprise huh?" She says to me, as we hug I tell her thank you but she could never know how important this is to me.

"Yes, I'm ready mom, I'm so ready!" I say to her.

CHAPTER 5

"Packed up and the car is loaded the moment of truth is here. The list says you can't have much; they'll give us everything that we will need. We are supposed to drive to a private airport, and they will take it from there. Dude, I am so excited about this thing, imagine me like some young super duper detective fighting machine. Oh yeah, I'm lighting right now, as we arrive my mother doesn't seem to worry this is a little strange for her."

"She doesn't say much, only smiles, well that is until I get out of the car then here goes the water works."

"Now you be on your best behavior, remember what we taught you, better not forget those manners. You kids really do grow up fast, make me proud okay?" She says to me with tears in her eyes, I let her know that I will. We hug and then Mr. Brown steps down off the plane, nice I just busted a rhyme. LOL!

"Mrs. Johnson, we will take good care of your son, don't you worry, are you ready Sedale?" He asks me, which is a real crazy question.

"Yes Sir, Roscoe you take care of Mom while I'm gone!" I say to my dog, rubbing his head then I hug my mother one last time then we get on the plane. I feel like a secret agent, here goes everything. I find my seat plane is empty but loaded with all kinds of things video games and junk food. I find a seat. I can see my mom and Roscoe we wave to each other as the plane begins to move to take off. Yep this is also my first plane flight, seatbelt light comes on above my head and then there is a pause and then WHOOOOSH!

"We go speeding down the runway and I am pushed back into my seat. Then I feel the plane take off as we begin to float a lot like I had imagined it would feel like."

"The plane cuts through the clouds, and then there is the blue sky, I feel so like the superhero that I have read so much about. I get to pick from whatever food and drink that I want."

"Chili Cheese Hotdog and tater tots, for me please, oh and lemonade soda!" I say to the lady, as I start playing some random video game. The food finally comes out and I eat till I'm about to bust, then I get sleepy. That meal sure was good. I guess I'll take a nap now.

"The pilot just told us that we will be landing in a couple of minutes didn't know I was asleep that long, and there goes the fasten your seatbelt sign again. I can feel the plane going down slowly and smoothly. It's pretty cool I wonder what will the landing will be like. I guess I'm about to find out, yep I just did smooth must be a good pilot; like I really know what a good pilot is, this is my first flight. We land and I get my stuff together and can't wait to start my training, I get off the plane and Mr. Brown is at the bottom waiting on me that guy is really fast I didn't even see him pass me."

"Hope you had a pleasant flight young man because you won't have comfort for a long time. Your training will test you and as you progress it will get tougher as you become more advanced, well let's go," Mr. Brown says.

"You know I've been thinking why did my mother let me go so easily. I'm gonna have to ask her about this, it's like she and Mr. Brown had planned this all along."

"I as ready as I'll ever be Sir, just need to pick up my things and we can go I guess?" I grab my bags and climb into the black Hum-V and fasten my seat belt because the car is making that annoying sound when you don't fasten your seat belt. As we drive away and from the airport, it gets really green around us like forest area from one of those fable books."

"Then I finally see it, the training area, and boy does it look wicked. You can see the people running around training in groups, jets fly overhead and all kinds of things."

"That is your unit Sedale get your things and join them. Those kids are you age group, Code name Delta Dogs. You will become a tight unit and then you'll see who is special and who is, well average," Mr. Brown says, I grab my things and run to the group, there is a big guy with a big hat looks pretty tough like he won't stand for any mess, well here goes the next 6 months."

"Hello, ladies I am Drill Sgt. Havoc, you are here to prove that you belong here, some of you mama's boys won't make it because you're gonna miss mommy wiping your butts and making your beds for you, making your dinners.

WRONG! There are no mommies here just me, and rest assure I won't wipe your butts. I will whip you into shape and ship most of you out, this is a privilege so don't get it twisted! SO DROP AND GIVE ME TWENTY, MOVE LUNCH MEAT'S!" Drill Sgt. Havoc says man, we all drop pretty quickly and some can't even do one push up and he doesn't cut them any slack."

"Then he tells everyone but the weak ones to follow him to our pods. He yells double time, I don't know what that means, none of us do as we stop and stand there."

Drill Sgt. Then explodes "MOVE LUNCH MEAT'S, THAT MEANS RUN!!"

"We all do down a hall way and to our rooms. He orders us to pick a bunk and, that lights will go out in 2 hours."

"Tomorrow you will hit it hard at 05:00 hours, so have your panties pressed lunch meat because then you belong to me!" Drill Sgt. Havoc says."

"I try to look around the pod to see who would be cool, to hang with, but I guess I will just wait I've changed my mind about it let me unpack. I'm gonna take the top bunk in case there is a bed wetter that wants to sleep above me, don't want a water bed. Everyone seems pretty upbeat and loud and then there is this!"

"LIGHTS OUT LADIES!" Drill Sgt. Havoc yells."

"Man, two hours sure came quick!" I think to myself.

"The next day I'm up at 4:45 am ready to go trying to get a jump on things, outta nowhere you hear a Drill Sgt. over the loud speaker every kid is either running, falling out of bed, tripping over things but ready. Some didn't even wash their faces or brush their teeth; boy that's nasty and I can hear my parents now about that."

"I can see what they mean when they say you will need these lessons when you are on your own, and what they are teaching me will put me ahead of the average kid. We hit the black top and warm up with push ups then sit ups, once we are done with them pulling the kids that can't do a single one of either we start on the 1 mile run which is supposed to get longer through out the week and months to follow."

"Like the push-ups and sit-ups some don't make it they "Fall out of the run" is what the Drill Sgt. calls it. Once we make it back to the pods we have to stand in the cold and man was it cold, now it's time for breakfast. To tell you the truth I'm not even hungry after all that exercise."

"We all line up but are told not to talk before we eat, this is really intense I wonder who will be the first one to test the Drill Sgt's. Good, no one was stupid we march in a straight line to the mess hall as they call it."

"Eyes forward and don't say a word or you'll be beating your face until your nose bleeds. NOW GET IT TOGETHER LUNCH MEAT'S!" A Drill Sgt. yells.

"We get our food and it tastes bad but I eat a little of it, they make us eat fast, and then back out side for the line up, it's back to work time for us. Rope climbing and more running the time has really gone by and before you know it's lunch, then dinnertime, same order line up and march. Food still tastes bad but this time, I'm hungry and I really eat."

"Then back to the Pods, and I am tired more tired than I've ever been but I like this challenge for some strange reason. We shower, then we get instructions for the next day. I look around and see that only a few kids are still game to keep going. I hear lights out and collapse on my bunk and I'm off to never, never land."

"GET UP LUNCH MEAT'S THIS AIN'T NO HOTEL MOVE, MOVE, MOVE!" A Drill Sgt. yells oh man he caught me sleeping."

"I was completely worn out, and so it went on like this for the next five months and the pod got really thin as kids got sent home to moms and dads. Pretty sad they didn't want it bad enough, well I do and in the last month, they started teaching us about, things that would help us fight the things that go thump in the night. What do you know? I see two familiar faces I can't believe it, Sterling and Dexter."

"What are you guys doing here I thought that you two got, got by the creepy guy well he's not so creepy after all." I say to them, as I am glad to see them as we walk to the class.

"Who, Mr. Brown? That guy is Boss what do you mean creepy?" Dexter asks.

"Well he was floating around the school grounds at first for awhile and he would just vanish it was weird, then he showed up at my home with my parents and offered me this chance to do big stuff," Sterling replies.

"Same here he just popped up outta nowhere for me also, when did you get the call, Sedale?" Dexter asks.

"On my birthday he showed up at my house talking to my mother, and he explained that something was taking the kids, something not quite human.

You know the ones that have been talked about on the news, I thought that he was the one and I thought he got you but man was I wrong this is the chance of a lifetime," I say to them both as we slap five and fist bump.

"How many flunked out of your pod we started with I can't remember but we are down to 13?" Dexter asks.

"Me either we have 10 left I saw many fail and whine like little girls heck some of the girls were tougher than the boys," Sterling adds.

"Two from my pod, me and that girl over there are all that are left from my pod, I tell you we are it, the ELITE!" I say as we are instructed to get to our seats to start the new lessons about what we are going to be facing once we finish our training.

This is where the good stuff starts, yes we still will be in training as far as running and we will still have our basic boring regular school stuff but here we go our instructor is just about to start the survival stuff.

"Students you are now about to take your first steps into war against the unknown, now what you will be learning with me are the many weapons against such foes. My name is Mrs. Oliver I have a great deal of experience in this field, you will learn the how's and why's of minerals, metals, liquids and in turn the affects they will have on your targets. Make no mistake, some of these targets are pretty nasty, and you will be in the battle quite often with nothing more than your wits, guile, and determination. This site started off with 1,000 students and 10 pods we are down to 2 pods with 25 of you in each on both sides, as you look around notice that there are faces that you won't recognize. Reason is your pods are sectioned into to smaller units 4 mainly some of you where right next to each other and had no idea." Mrs. Oliver says, think man, that many in that many out.

We all look around intensely, and realize that we are pretty lucky or determined to be here but if we are still here, then we must really want to be here. Still I can't help but think who wouldn't try with all their hearts not to want to be here.

"The first mineral we are going to talk about is salt, it has been around as long as the earth and it seems to have a profound effect on a great deal of creatures here or extra dimensional. It can be used in many forms, rock salt, a liquid mixture, or in basic table salt form," Mrs. Oliver adds.

"Mrs. Oliver do you have an example of how this is used, I've seen it put on snails and they shrivel up?" Sterling asks.

"Well there are creatures with the same body composition similar to the snail, but let's just use for example the supernatural. Have you ever seen a person take a pinch of salt and throw it over their shoulder?" Mrs. Oliver questions.

"Yes I have my grandmother used to do that all the time, she said it keeps away ghosts. I thought she was just crazy or something," Dexter responds.

"Well she is absolutely right but it will only do that to evil spirits, they cannot stand nor can they break a salt line because salt is one of the purest things we have on earth, it disrupts their negative link to our realm. She was not crazy, trust me, she just had knowledge of the creatures that lurk about us undetected by the naked eye," Mrs. Oliver says.

Our classes went on like this week after week. We were asked many questions and shown many ways to use things like salt, silver, and iron as weapons. How to use everyday things to apply them to fight with, even showed us how to make delivery systems for them.

I am having the time of my life as I take all this in, I've passed every PT test and exam and I'm feeling really good about stopping the baddies.

Sterling and Dexter seem like they are having the time of their lives here also, we now head for lunch and we actually get to talk to each other now, even sit together. So as we do I strike up the conversation, it's good to see friends especially when you think they got snatched.

"Fellas it's really good to see you, man when I didn't see you in class first Dexter then Sterling did a no show I thought I'd never see you bums again," I say.

"Well, I didn't have the same feelings I never knew that you guys thought I was missing. It was real sudden, who would have thought that this was such a place it's like the Outer Limits or X-Files you know?" Dexter replies.

"Well it was kinda creepy when you didn't show up at school after the battle of the video games, we really thought you were a goner!" Sterling answers.

"When both of you stopped coming that's when it just got too weird for words, I wonder what the other kids back home are thinking. They told me that we can't talk about this to anyone other than our parents, so the kids at school must be really trippin? Did they tell you guys that you can't talk about this?" I ask them.

"Yeah, they said that this stuff is like above top, top secret and this is how they have kept it quiet for so long. I feel like Jason Borne, I'm a real bad butt!" Dexter responds.

"The same, their training really brought out the 3 muscles that I had times 5 over. Check this out!" Sterling says as he tries to bust a bodybuilding pose. Dexter shoots milk out of his nose laughing so hard.

"Oh it burns, it burns, Sterling that is the most awful thing I've ever seen, I thought Larry Bird retired put that bird back in its cage please!" Dexter says.

"Yeah Ster, looks like you been trying to go for a week and nothings happening, keep that up and you'll blow a hole in your shorts!" I say to him, as Dexter and I are rolling with laughter.

"Aw you guys are a bunch of haters, ya'll are just jealous of my Luke Cage body, I put in a lot of work on this bod!" Sterling responds as the tears are rolling down our faces.

"You look like a shaved Quail, man enough already!" Dexter says jokingly.

"Oh man, I needed that laugh, been a long time since I laughed that hard, we should make a commitment to stay tight for life what do you cat's say?" I ask as I extend my hand and then the two meatheads pile their hands on top of mine and shout "Tight for life!" and a new gang is born. We finish eating and then it's off to class we have one more PT test next week then we graduate and then back to the real world with our new knowledge. From now on guys we are 3D."

"Mrs. Oliver, may I have a word with you?" Washington Brown asks as she stops to listen.

"Those 3 are going to be special, started off as enemies and now they are best friends; we need to put them on different assignments and see how they fare. This way we can assess what kind of team they could become if unified," Mr. Brown says.

"You are right. smart, strong, loyal, this makes for a great beginning. Haven't seen this kind of thing in a long time, most just wash out.

They even avoided the food traps in the cafeteria, foods like ice cream, potato chip, sodas, and candy. All the things that would slow reflexes slow down, PT scores, and dull the mind. Pretty amazing," Mrs. Oliver responds.

"Sedale's mother says that he is all about the junk food, pizza, hamburgers, sodas, and the other two's parents said the same about them. But yet they didn't fall for any of the traps, not one of the three. That Sedale has the makings of a great leader, the boy has guts to spare; I have the perfect first assignment for him when he gets out of here," Mr. Brown says.

"I think I know what you have in mind, that thing that's been taking the kids in his town right? Have you figured out what it is yet?" Mrs. Oliver asks, as Mr. Brown raises an eyebrow and answers her.

"Yes, I'll shoot you an email, give the other two the easier tasks I want to make sure they keep their confidence, but Sedale is the one most suited to lead them. I want to test him and see if I'm right!" Mr. Brown says.

"Okay, I will get right on it. Next week is their last week and I'll have those tasks ready before then. Just have to find the right homes in the right neighborhoods with the most activity," Mrs. Oliver replies.

"Good, I will see you later. This has the makings of something special!" Mr. Brown says as he nods and tips his hat to Mrs. Oliver, they part company.

"Final week: we all pass the tests. Me, Dexter, and Sterling's team manage to be the last team who was much bigger in Tug of War I don't know how but we just wouldn't quit until they were swimming in mud.

Sterling was screaming like he had a lot of pinned up emotions inside, I watched as the Drill Sgts. looked at him, then at each other and nodded in approval to his explosion of emotions."

"The next day they have us in separate rooms and we wait for the go or no go and they tell us what our first assignments are going to be. My hands are sweating, they don't want us together, each assignment is for each person only. I'm ready even though my leg is shaking, I wonder how Dexter and Sterling are doing, hopefully not posing, I say to myself jokingly!"

"Then it is my turn and in walks Mrs. Oliver, with papers and some other stuff."

"Well it seems like you are the last on my list, we have shown you how to use slingshots, bow, and arrows, along with an assortment of many firing weapons. Now to the task at hand, you will be facing a creature that is inter dimensional. it is call the 'Mo Ja,' which means the 'Closet Walker.' This thing is very evasive and deadly, don't worry you won't be trapping a full grown one, you will be facing an adolescent one. They are very impatient and act on pure aggression, which makes them clumsy, and mistake prone. Pull this off and you are on your way to lead others, make no mistake this will be a dangerous endeavor. Now I'm sure you have many questions so now is the time to ask!" Mrs. Oliver says, and boy do I have a lot of questions.

"Mrs. Oliver ma'am what does these 'MoJa' want, how many are there, do we know what they look like, and how do we stop them?" I ask.

"To your first question, they like just about everything the human body can provide, mostly heat, because in their dimension it's rather cold and the human body has a chemical that will generate heat long after it is gone. Children are the biggest targets for these things, children generate the heat chemical especially when afraid, so they have figured this fact out and target your kind. The closet is where they attack from, it's mostly dark in closets and they cannot stand the light one bit.

"Keeping the light on stops them, but not everyone knows that they are there and some parents are unwilling to leave the light on for their children feeling that it will make them too accustomed in the long run and slow their development." Mrs. Oliver says.

"Bed wetter's, right. Without light, a lot of kids won't go to the bathroom for fear of a monster getting them. I was one of those kids, it always felt like something was waiting for me. I stayed jumpy. I got a lot of spankings back then too, I wouldn't even go with out waking my dad to take me," I respond.

"Well I suppose you might have been right to feel that way many other things pray on kids in the darkness at night, and most of the time when you feel like you are not alone you are not. The 'MoJa' has no apparent head or neck, just a long face, broad shoulders, a wide mouth, long arms that drag the floor and hoofed feet that support a long wide torso. They have powerful legs that allow them to move with blur-like quickness, they attack when one's back is turned and unsuspecting. They grab hold bite down and drain whatever they need at the time from their prey and drag them off to their world. That person is never seen again, what is said that their realm has bodies floating in a vacuum-less black void slowly decaying. The last thing a person will see is the green glow from its eyes." Mrs. Oliver says.

"This is just one of the treats you will be facing, oh one other thing it will be invisible until it strikes but the air is distorted where it moves. Humans are the one race that can detect when they come around, choose your weapons wisely, find a way to make it seen before they attack, remember the young ones are sloppy and are forced to fend for themselves shortly after they are born and abandoned." Mrs. Oliver ads, she seems really confident in me. That helps calm me a little bit.

"I'm already thinking of a way to make it seen and trap it, just show me the way to where it is I will bag it for you, Mrs. Oliver," I reply.

"We have a fake mother and father family setting, picked out for you so that you can make your move. Nice home but it's all fake to lure the creature out.

We will have them leave you home alone and that's when it will make its move, it has really been active in this area. The address is 345 Oak Tree Dr.

Now gather your things if you have no further questions, your flight awaits,"

Mrs. Oliver says to me as she hands me a DVD and notes even though I took my own notes.

"Mrs. Oliver, who exactly are we; I mean who are we supposed to be group wise?" I ask, she stops for a moment and gives a strange answer.

"Have you heard of The Men in Black, not the movies, but the real ones? Think of yourselves as the junior team, only you will do the job they hesitate to do, you will learn more in time. Now if you have no more questions, I suggest you go catch your plane!" Mrs. Oliver responds to me as she walks away.

I do the same; grabbing my things and going to my airplane and Dexter and Sterling are boarding their planes. All they do is wave to me as the doors shut on their planes. Mr. Brown, who gives me words of encouragement, meets me.

"Your time to shine young man, you unified those guys who would have been enemies for years to come. Don't think that you will be facing this task alone, you will be monitored but help will only come when and if you are in grave danger. Here is your badge of course completion, good luck!" Mr. Brown says.

"Here I thought you were a weirdo, sir, and you just opened the door to a world I thought was just in the movies. I won't let you down, sir, I will complete the job you can believe it!" I respond, and we shake hands as I board my plane. I can see Sterling's and Dexter's planes take off, man it looks so cool up close but now to the real deal. I put on my head phones and put the DVD Mrs. Oliver gave me and learn more about my mission, call me Jr. James Bond, minus the women. I'm not ready for them yet, they are scarier than the MoJa.

CHAPTER 6

"I've contacted your mother and let her know that you have you first assignment, then you go home for a little while," Mr. Brown says.

"How is she doing is she holding up okay my dad's always away and our dog is the only company she has?" I respond, but when I mention my dad being away often I noticed that Mr. Brown raised an eyebrow.

"She's fine, and believe it or not your dad was with her and is leaving as we speak. He sends his congratulations and love," Mr. Brown replies, oh man did I want to see my dad and show him how much I've changed.

'Boy, guess I'll have to catch 'em on the rebound, glad mom's okay too, lots of stuff I been going over and I'm hungry, when do we eat?" I ask.

"You just ate and hour ago, where do you put it all, but let me get the cooks on it," Mr. Brown replies, he leaves his seat and I get a video picture on my phone from Sterling and Dexter at the same time. You gotta love hi-tech stuff.

"What's up fellas got my mission how about you cats?" I ask.

"I've got mine," Dexter answers while stuffing his face.

"Me too but we are not supposed to talk about it to each other," Sterling says with sunglasses on really trying to look cool sipping on soda.

"Well let me be the first to say I'm nervous!" I say to them.

"Me too!" Sterling responds.

"Ditto!" Dexter says.

"Well nice chatting with you two girls but now I'm gonna kick back and relax until I get to my mission D-money out. Oh, before I forget check out this feed from MonsterQuest, this Bigfoot is slamming this lady's head against the steering wheel and it's making the horn go off. It's hilarious, well at least I thought so!" Dexter adds as his video feed ends.

"Well Sedale, Dex, I gotta go, these women treat me like I'm famous and I don't want to jinx my mojo so holla dolla's. Yes ma'am more juice please!" Sterling says not realizing that he still had his feed going, Holla Dolla's? Wow, what an attempt at trying to be cool, that Sterling is something else.

"I guess I should do the same, get my mind ready, this is my first mission challenge, but first let me tear up this sweet and sour chicken with fried rice first then I'll catch a nap. Excuse me may I have some apple cranberry please, and thank you?"

"Sedale, Sedale wake up I'd like for you to meet your parents well artificial, parental, tactical, guides A.P.T.G. They are going to be what lures the MoJa out they are going to leave you home alone without a protector. The area and house are very nice, almost a mansion that we have selected. Here agents Mr. Robert Smalls and Ms. Marry Vines. Your temporary chaperones," Mr. Brown says as he wakes me up, man already their jets are quick. They sure don't look like agents, just average parents; they really have this thing thought out.

"Pleased to meet you Sir and…" I'm stopped by Ms. Peaks before I can get her greeting out!

"Don't you dare say that M-word makes me feel old Mary is cool!" she says to me, boy she is really pretty though not too fat not too skinny. Okay, that's what I was hoping for, a smile. For a minute there I thought she was gonna be a Meany. Mr. Smalls looks like he lifts weights and has a happy go lucky look on his face.

"Are you ready Sedale; we are almost to the house, about three hours till sundown?" he asks.

"Yes sir, can't wait to get started, time to show what I know!" Did I just try to rap? Oh boy, Sterling is rubbing off on me.

"Well you have really nice manners, you must have good parents, not many kids have them anymore great to see that," he answers.

"Yes, sir the best! Can't wait to make them proud!" I reply with pride in my folks.

"I wished you good luck earlier prematurely but now I do at the proper time, we are here at our post," Mr. Brown says, we pull up and it is a huge house. I grab my gear and get out of the car, while I follow everybody one in trying to act like the adults around me. They really seem calm like they've done this a thousand times before.

"So now I guess this is how it's gonna go down. I will go through this in the steps in order. We go in after Mr. Brown, who shakes my hand and pats me on the back. The cameras and other fancy things are set up ahead of time so all I have to do is check my gear, okay, mega-pressure water gun check, I filled it with the glow stick light water or whatever it is.

I also got oil and salt in separate balloons each for my defense trip wires, well its really just fishing line. Sling shot and golf balls. I scored the highest with the slingshot of all that attended the camp, and I love this thing.

Then the two agents and I fake like we are a family. I pretend like I'm doing homework, which I actually am while they do things like check out the sports channel and other things that adults would do. It gets a bit later and they plan to get out to see a movie. I continue to check out the house for attack points, boy there are a bunch of closets in this place.

"I think I will take the one closest to the huge T.V. Down stairs in the den and my upstairs pretend bedroom."

"Note to self: I have been feeling that little prickly feeling on the back of my neck, which is very creepy man. From the notes I have this means that we have company. So the two agents, before they leave, give me the final details."

"So Sedale do you see this spot on the floor right at the bottom of the stairs? That's where you need to get the MoJa it and hit that button on the wall, now look up, that net matted against the ceiling is made of a silver and lead compound. It will not be able to get back to its dimension and then we can come in and haul it off. I don't have to tell you to be careful, this will be dangerous." Mr. Smalls says, and that really makes me a bit nervous.

"I think you got this though so if it gets to where you can't handle it hit the emergency button on your belt and the team outside will be in here post haste," Mary adds. Well, I do feel a bit better but I've got to do this on my own.

"They hug me and leave as I lock the door and get ready for this terror task. I play a few video games and junk food then the floor creeks from the kitchen area so I pause the game to look in that direction."

"What do you know nothing, yeah right this thing must think I'm stupid? So I stop and turn on the Monster Mayhem series microwave some popcorn then I'm set."

"Out of the corner of my eye I see a distortion and then a dark shadow streaks by but as I look to where I saw it last it's gone. So it's here, at the bottom of the stairway, there is no carpet above the net drop, and there is none that leads from my fake bedroom. I turn and look back at the T.V. I've got to lure this thing out into the open. So I fake like I'm dozing off, and then it begins."

"About 10 minutes after I turn out the lights I feel something in the room with me but I don't respond or panic I just play it cool. Then I see really long skinny fingers coming over the back of the couch, they look like they're covered with spider webs, that's when I make my move. I lean forward just as the Monster tries to get me. I hop over the table and face my foe, it looks awful, well for brief second I can see it poping in and out of open space. It lunges for me I move and it is caught in the T.V. light. It lets out a scream that I have to cover my ears, it is something I will never forget as it bangs its head against the floor and with one swipe it totals the huge flat screen T.V."

"Still it gives me time to run upstairs to regroup. I take my gear and head to my fake bedroom. I lock the door and turn on the light while taking cover behind the bed. I look on my shoulders and there is this weird glow like it dripped something on me, this is how it marks you so that it can hunt you till it gets you! "Well not today, ugly I won't be your meal!" I yell this out and it's really quiet and wouldn't you know it the power goes out. Then the closet door has a weird glowing red mist coming from it as it slowly opens, creaking."

"Then I take my tools out, as a nasty looking hand slowly pushes the door open a low growl is coming from the door slowly opening also. Then the mist gets bigger it's got little flashes of light sparking in it, you know like a small thunder cloud. My skin feels all charged, the blankets are sticking to me as I try to stay out of sight. The MoJa busts through the door shattering it, wood is flying all over the room. I put on my night vision goggles but they won't work, dang must be all the static in the air."

"I feel the floor shake as the Moja is coming to me, so I just throw two of my special balloons one filled with oil and the other with glow stick liquid light at it. BULL's EYE RIGHT! Now I can see this thing and boy talk about ugly, eyes where the shoulders should be and a big nasty mouth in the middle of where a belly should be full of pointed teeth. It's having a hard time moving because of the oil balloon bomb I hit it with, but it comes at me fast, I move out of the way with my gear-filled backpack. I run to the bathroom across the hall and shut the two doors behind me, I think I'm safe for the moment then I hear the door outside crash. Oh boy, I'm just a lil' scared, gotta get my confidence up."

"Hey, you ain't gonna get me you crack sniffin' butt muncher. You have met your match this time!" I yell as I slam three more of my oil-filled balloons on the floor by the door. Then I back up to the other door of the bathroom that leads to the hallway on the other side, turn to run out and you guessed, it comes crashing through the wall. This time, to its surprise it's met by oil slipping. The Moja slams into the bathtub. I take the lid off the back of the toilet and pop its ugly skull until the lid shatters.

"I see you like knots on your head snake lips, there is more where that came from let's go Mojo!" I shout as it tries to grab me but too slow, don't you know. I run out and into the hallway locking the door behind me. I check out my next point of attack. I've just got to stand in this spot let it just get close enough to where it thinks it can grab me and BAM trap it easy, peezy. Top of the stairs hardwood floor think, Sedale, think! I throw down the last of my oil balloons on that spot and rub it all over the spot and some on my arms and legs. Now I just need to wait for its next move, since it's not invisible it can't be sneaky.

"Come on duffus, what are ya waitin' for, I ain't running from you anymore," funny thing is, it won't take the bait. I guess I have to sweeten the meal.

I can play opossum-like I'm hurt or something a wounded animal, I've read no predator can resist. So I take off my shirt and rub more oil on my arms and back, and legs then I lie on the floor and start whimpering like I'm hurt. It starts to work as I hear the floors creaking all over the house which is kind of weird, just got to hold on until the thing makes its attack. I'm gonna moan louder with my head in my hands but just enough where I can still see around me.

"Then the floor and pictures on the walls start shaking, and there is this weird humming all around me, just like that, it all stops. I look over my shoulder and the door to the bathroom explodes. I cover my head with my hands to protect me from splinters, and as I look back the smoke clears a little then I see the glow stick covered hands and feet of the monster that hunts children. It comes for me. I crawl, pretending I'm injured, that's all it took because now it starts walking towards me fast."

"The Moja tries to grab my leg but it can't get a grip because of the oil, so it tries to grab my long shorts. I didn't count on it doing this, it pulls me back trying to, I guess, take me into its realm. I kick it hard in the eye and one hand lets me go, as it grunts and covers the eye, but it still keeps pulling me. I roll back onto my stomach and reach for my backpack, grab a little salt and throw it over my left shoulder in the same eye that I kicked. The monster bellows out and starts slamming its body into the side of the wall. I didn't think that salt would mess it up like this, well thank goodness for education.

I look up and right above the creature I notice a trap set that I can use against the Moja. There is a string that says pull me. Odd, I jump all over it and pull the string."

"A spring-loaded sledgehammer comes flying out of the ceiling and knocks the monster into the back wall hard. Still it won't stop but it is definitely next to the top of the stairs where I need it to be. I throw my balloon that is filled with salt at it, this time, the whole monster is covered and screaming as the salt burns its meat. I make a dash and slide between its legs as it tries to get me, then I shove it as hard as I can. the Moja slips on the oil covered spot and falls down the stairs to the bottom.

It's trying to get up, I realize I've got one last chance to finish this my sling shot and golf balls. I've got to hit the button on the wall to release the silver-coated net to trap it. The bottom of the stairs is solid hardwood the best surface now I toss my last bomb balloon, now the MoJa can't stand it's slipping and sliding all over the place scratching up the wall and rail."

"Now to get my aim right, and fire, oh snap darn creature stands up, the golf ball hits it in the skull, one shot left, my hands are oily and I just missed with my last golf ball shot. I'm out of choices now. I look around as the monster tries hard to get the burning salt off of it. Before it comes to its senses I got one choice left so I jump and slide down the stairs arm rail, with my big water gun still filled I slide by the Moja as it is flinging its arms like a mad rooster. I throw my gun and hit the button; the net comes falling down on top of the creature, as I slam hard into the wall. OUCH! Boy did that hurt, lucky I've got a hard head."

"The creature seems dead like the silver has killed it but I know that ain't true, it's just having an allergic reaction to the silver. I step closer to take a look and this thing Is ugggly plus it stinks P.U. Just then it reaches for me and I jump out of the way, that was a close one. I go to the main room checking for bruises and press the signal for team to come get this thing. I strut to the fridge like a tough guy, grab me a can of cold lemonade and sit down on the couch. I feel really good first mission in the bag. Not to bad for a twelve-year-old, I wonder how Dexter and Sterling did on their missions."

"I gotta say though I was a bit scared thank God I pulled it off."

"Doesn't take long for the team to get here, maybe five minutes, they tag and bag the MoJa. Mr. Washington Brown comes in to shake my hand."

"Great job son, your parents, are going to be very proud, you are one of only 3 that have pulled this off without assistance since the start of this program many decades ago let's get you home," Mr. Brown says, as I stand up and shake his hand.

"Yes sir, thank you, sir," I respond as we shake hands.

"Don't thank me, thank your parents, you have great ones who didn't take short cuts in your upbringing. Being a parent is not a part time gig, it's a full-time job. Too many parents have forgotten that fact," Mr. Brown says.

"Thank you, sir, I have the best parents! I reply, I can't help but think that he knows more about my parents than he's telling me but that's another story I guess."

"I've learned so much in my last couple of months about myself, my friends and things that go bump in the night. There are some things that a parent can't protect us from or themselves from, well at least not completely. Sterling and Dexter are now friends, Dexter taught us both a good lesson about bullies: sometimes they do have benefits. Sheep or Shepherd, which do you choose to be? This story, my friend was told from the eyes of a kid, a smart kid. I may not have all the fancy big words to explain things but you get the point."

"Wait Mr. Brown is coming back, I bet it's a medal or the newest game system, an extra reward?"

"Oh one last thing Sedale here is your next assignment," Mr. Brown says, as my eyes get wide as I look at the computer pad he hands me.

"MR. BROWN YOU'RE KIDDING ME RIGHT!?! NO WAY THESE THINGS ARE REAL?"

Printed in the United States
By Bookmasters